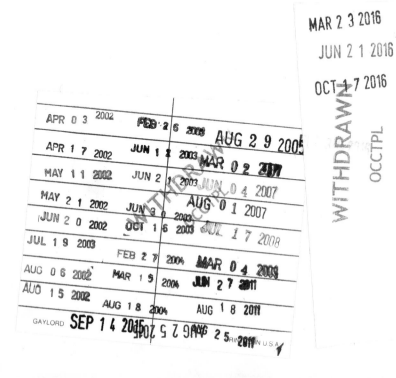

All Growed-Up!

KLASKY CSUPO INC.

Based on the TV series *Rugrats*® created by Arlene Klasky, Gabor Csupo, and
Paul Germain as seen on Nickelodeon®

SIMON SPOTLIGHT
An imprint of Simon & Schuster Children's Publishing Division
1230 Avenue of the Americas
New York, New York 10020

Manufactured in the United States of America

First Edition
2 4 6 8 10 9 7 5 3 1

ISBN 0-689-84413-1

Rugrats

All Growed-Up!

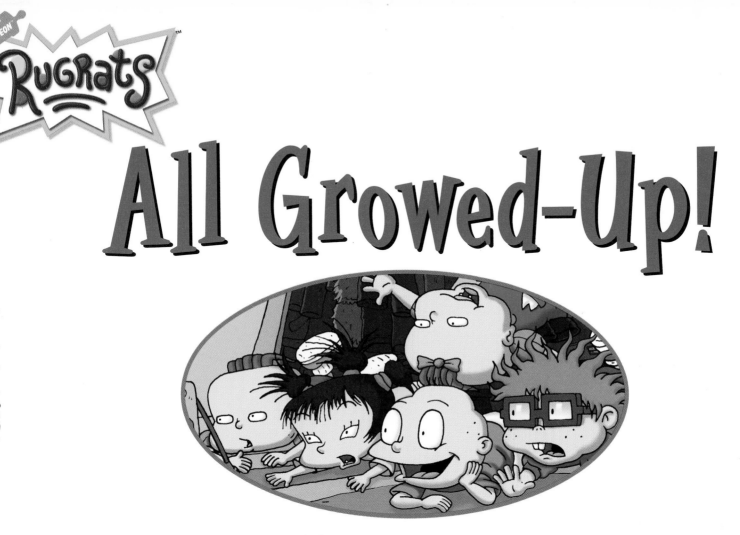

adapted by Cathy West

from the script by Kate Boutilier and Eryk Casemiro

illustrated by Jim Durk

Simon Spotlight/Nickelodeon

New York   London   Toronto   Sydney   Singapore

"Hurry, Chuckie!" Tommy Pickles called out. "Professor Spooky is gonna put a boy into the foocher on TB!"

"Wow," Tommy said. "Wouldn't it be neat to go to the foocher?"

"I don't know, Tommy," said Chuckie. "What if the foocher gots even more scary things than the right-now?"

Tommy patted Chuckie's shoulder. "It wouldn't be scary, Chuckie. 'Cause we'd be biggerer."

"And smarterer," said Kimi.

But Chuckie still looked worried.

Angelica stomped in front of the TV. "This is my new tapiokey machine," she bragged. "I gots a show to do, and you diaper bags are gonna be my applaudience!" She pressed a button and music began to play.

"Oh, beeyooteeful for spaceship eyes . . . ," Angelica belted out.

"Is it my imagination, or is Angelica getting louderer?" whispered Phil.

"I didn't think Angelica *could* be louderer," Lil answered.

"For purple mounds of majesty above the fruited rain!" continued Angelica, knocking over everything in sight.

"Hey, Angelica," Tommy said. "Can I try your—"

"NO!" shouted Angelica. "Dumb babies can't play with my stuffs!" And she huffed off.

"It's not fair, you guys," Tommy said with a scowl. "Angelica always plays with *our* new toys."

"You heard her, Tommy," Chuckie warned. "We're not opposed to play with it."

Tommy picked up the microphone and punched a button. "HELLO?" he said loudly. "Testing, one, two, . . . LA-LA-LA-LA-LA—"

"HEY!" Angelica shouted. "What do you think you're doing, bald-brain?"
"Ruuuuuuuun!" Chuckie cried.
The babies scattered, dragging the karaoke machine along with them.

Hiding in a closet nearby, the babies held on to the doorknob with all their might.

"GIVE ME BACK MY TAPIOKEY MACHINE!" Angelica shrieked as she tugged from the other side.

"What are we going to do?" gasped Chuckie.

"I don't know," Tommy said, "but I'm tired of Angelica bossing us around. She treats us like a bunch of babies!"

"Well, we're not eggsackly growed-ups yet," Chuckie pointed out.

"That's it!" Tommy cried. "We'll go to the foocher! We'll be so growed-up, Angelica won't be able to boss us around."

"But we don't gots a time machine like Professor Spooky," Phil said.

"Sure we do!" Tommy cried. He found an old jump rope in the back of the closet and jabbed one end into a deflated basketball. Then he attached the other end to the karaoke machine.

Suddenly the closet shook. A bright light flashed. "Hang on, everybody!" Tommy yelled.

The babies tumbled out of the closet . . . and into the future!
But so did Angelica. "Hand over my new Emica CD!" she shouted.
"But you said we could borrow it," Tommy said.
Angelica snatched the CD from Tommy's hand. "Too bad!"

Tommy's dad boogied his way into the kitchen, stopping to strike a pose.

"Oh, Stu, the memories are flooding back!" Didi gushed.

"Uh . . . , Dad, I don't remember you wearing *that*!" Dil pointed to the large gold Scorpio medallion hanging from his father's neck.

"Solid gold-plated," Stu said proudly. "I was wearing it the night I met your mom," he added. "It's my good-luck charm. I can't dance without it."

"We're going to dance in the Dinosaurs of Disco contest tomorrow night at the park," Didi explained as Stu twirled her around.

As the kids scrambled into the school bus, Angelica hurried to sit with her best friend, Samantha.

"Hey, Angelica, save Chuckie and me a seat!" Tommy shouted. But Angelica looked right past him as if she couldn't see him.

"Check out this cool necklace!" Samantha said.

Angelica stared in disbelief. Emica's necklace looked just like her Uncle Stu's Scorpio medallion! "I have the same one," Angelica blurted out. "And I'm gonna to wear it to the concert tomorrow night."

"Emica always chooses someone to sing onstage with her," Samantha said. "You're sure to get picked wearing that necklace!"

Chuckie leaned over his seat. He had a strange crumpled look on his face.

"What's wrong?" Tommy asked.

"Samantha almost smiled at me," Chuckie whispered. "I tried to smile back, but my lips got stuck on my new braces." He sighed. "I feel kind of sick—but in a good way."

Wow, Tommy thought. Could Chuckie be . . . *in love?*

At lunchtime Chuckie saw Samantha again. He patted down his hair. Chuckie tried to smile, but it looked more like a weird grimace. "Eww!" Samantha gasped as she hurried past.

"So . . . ," Angelica whispered to Tommy. "*Your* best friend has a crush on *my* best friend." She smiled slyly. "I have a proposition to make. I'll tell Samantha what a great guy Chuckie is—*if* you get me Uncle Stu's Scorpio necklace. Deal?"

Tommy watched Chuckie dash off to a corner and bury his face in his hands. "Deal," Tommy groaned.

Tommy knew his dad wouldn't let him borrow the necklace. So he came up with another plan. He'd make a fake. Tommy took some gold foil and wrapped it around a dog biscuit. Then he traced a Scorpio design on top. "Angelica will get the real one," he told Dil. "Dad will get the fake."

"He'll be really mad if he finds out," Dil warned.

"I know," Tommy said. "But I have to do this for Chuckie!"

Tommy sneaked into his dad's room. He took the real gold necklace and left the fake one in its place. Then he tiptoed out.

Spike awoke with a start. He smelled his favorite treat—Tasty Pooch Snacks. He sniffed high and low, and then he ate the fake necklace in one big gulp!

The next morning Tommy put the real necklace on the kitchen table while he rooted around for his Reptar cereal. Spike spotted the necklace, grabbed it in his mouth, and ran outside.

The yard was littered with bits of gold foil. "Oh, no! Look!" Tommy moaned. "Spike must have eaten the fake necklace and then thought the real one was a dog treat too!"

"How will I dance without my lucky charm?" Stu cried when Tommy told him what had happened.

"Why would you take it without asking?" Didi asked.

Angelica had just come in. She shot Tommy a warning look.

"I . . . uh . . . wanted to wear it to the Emica concert so she'd invite me to sing onstage," Tommy fibbed.

"You're grounded," Stu said.

"You'll have to miss the concert," Didi said with a sigh.

"I can't believe you're grounded," Kimi said.

"What a bummer," said Phil as he pulled something out of the sand. "Cool! A Reptar pop!" He popped it into his mouth. "Circa 2001, I'd say."

Just then Spike started digging around in the sandbox.

"Hey, what's this?" Lil said, and pulled out—

"My dad's necklace!" Tommy cried. But his parents were already on their way to the dance contest.

Tommy and his friends hopped onto their bikes and sped off. Tommy hoped it wasn't too late to get his dad's lucky charm to him. But on the way through the park, Angelica spotted Tommy.

"You found the necklace!" Angelica cried as she lunged for it.

"You can't have it," Tommy said. "If Samantha can't see what a great guy Chuckie is without you telling her, she doesn't deserve him."

"C'mon!" Angelica begged. "Just let me wear it for a minute!"

"Not until you start telling the truth," Tommy demanded.

"What's *he* doing with *your* necklace?" Samantha asked.

Angelica locked eyes with Tommy then she sighed. "He's my cousin," she admitted. "It's his dad's necklace. He was just gonna let me borrow it."

"Oh, I see," Samantha said. Then she noticed Chuckie. He smiled a great big silver grin. "Don't I know you?" she asked.

"You should!" Angelica blurted. "Samantha Shane, meet Chuckie—I mean, Charles Finster."

Samantha smiled. "Braces were the worst!" she said. "You know, you're going to be really cute when your braces come off. Come on. Let's all go sit together."

"Nah, I'll see you guys later," Angelica said.

"What?!" Samantha exclaimed. "And miss Emica?"

Angelica shrugged. "I gotta take care of something."

By the time Tommy, Dil, and Angelica got to the Dinosaurs of Disco contest, Stu and Didi were on the dance floor. Stu was bumping and swiveling in all the wrong places.

"Okay, Dil," Angelica said as she handed him the necklace. "Make this one count!" Dil threw the necklace toward his dad.

Astonished, Stu caught it—and his rhythm returned. Stu and Didi began to dance like the king and queen of disco!

The kids made it back to the concert just in time for the last song.

"I'm going to need a little help for this next one!" Emica shouted. The spotlight circled the crowd and then stopped on Tommy.

"Pick me too!" Angelica shouted. "Please, please, please! I'm his cousin—and his agent!" They ran up onto the stage together and began to sing with their favorite star.

Angelica grabbed the mike.

Tommy tugged back. "It's still my turn!"

"You're forgetting who the star in the family is," Angelica said.

While they wrestled over the mike, a photographer took their picture and—FLASH!

Tommy and his friends tumbled out of the Pickleses' closet.

"Hey! You broked my tapiokey machine!" Angelica shouted. "You dumb babies better keep your mitts off my stuff for the next bazillion years!"

"Look on the bright side," Tommy told his friends. "Only ten more years till Angelica's nice to us."